RETCH

DAVID BERNSTEIN

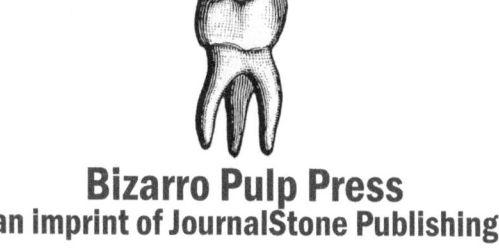

Bizarro Pulp Press
an imprint of JournalStone Publishing

This is a work of fiction. All of the characters, names, incidents, organizations, and dialogue in this novel are either the products of the author's imagination or are used fictitiously.

Bizarro Pulp Press books may be ordered through booksellers or by contacting:

Bizarro Pulp Press, a JournalStone imprint
    www.BizarroPulpPress.com

    ISBN: 978-1-945373-23-7

Printed in the United States of America
JournalStone rev. date: July 10, 2016

Cover Art: Justin T. Coons
Interior Formatting by: Lori Michelle
    www.theauthorsalley.com

PRAISE FOR DAVID BERNSTEIN

"An in-your-face, take-no-prisoners romp in the vein of Richard Laymon and Edward Lee"
—Examiner.com on *Goblins*

"A fascinating, unpredictable, ever-shifting tale of greed and desperation. Highly recommended!"
—Jeff Strand,
author of *Pressure on Relic of Death*

"Reminiscence of early '80s camp flicks."
—Horror Novel Reviews on *Witch Island*

"I mixed a pot of fake puke at home and then I went to this movie theater, hid the puke in my jacket, climbed up to the balcony and then, t-t-then, I made a noise like this: hua-hua-hua-huaaaaaaa —and then I dumped it over the side, all over the people in the audience. And then, this was horrible, all the people started getting sick and throwing up all over each other. I never felt so bad in my entire life."

—Chunk, from *The Goonies*

CHAPTER 1

THE WOMAN WAS wobbly-legged drunk when Brian left the club with her. His personal driver was outside in a Lincoln Town Car waiting for him. He and the woman, Daphne something or other, were taken to Brian's penthouse apartment located on the upper west side of Manhattan. The building was home to some of the city's wealthiest people.

Brian didn't care if Serge, the night doorman, saw him with a drunken commoner. The man was well paid by Brian and the rest of the building's residents. Paid for his duties, but also to forget things he may have witnessed. The goings on that occurred in wealthy circles tended to remain in wealthy circles. If not, people like Serge lost their jobs.

Brian was a hedge fund manager for Sky National Investment Bank. He traveled the world for business and pleasure, ate in the most select, high end restaurants, had a 24 hour driver at his beck and call, and could basically purchase any damn thing he desired.

He was a good-looking, twenty-nine-year old, single man who at times grew bored with how easy life had become. With one phone call, he could have whatever he wanted at his doorstep. His being single was by choice. Women constantly threw themselves at him. His parents—who resided in France, England, New Zealand, Manhattan, and California, depending on the time of year—had attempted on numerous occasions to set him up. Brian always found the women hollow and soulless, interested in living the way they had been raised and taught. A follow-the-numbers lifestyle. Keeping money with money. It disgusted him. No way in fucking hell was he going to have an arranged marriage, one where how they appeared in public was the most important part of the relationship. What was the point? He was better off being single.

Besides his morals, at heart, he was a player. He loved women and enjoyed sleeping with a different one every few days. The Commoners, as he referred to them, were his type. As long as they were hot they could be younger or older—MILFs were often the best fucks around. He got a thrill out of showing off his lifestyle, giving false promises and then ripping the rug out from under his subjects. What moronic female would actually think someone like him would fall in love with her and sweep her off her feet? Kicking them to the curb after he was done with them, usually the next morning, but sometimes that very night, was more satisfying than raking in a killing in the stock market.

He wasn't sure why he was such a bastard, but often wondered. Had it been the way he was raised? His environment? Being so good-looking and successful? He didn't think any of those were the case. It was most likely due to how he'd had his heart broken at the tender age of twenty by the commoner Mindy Sachs, having walked in on her fucking his old man. He'd threatened to tell his mother, ruin his father's life. But the man had spoken to him not in anger or embarrassment, but as a caring dad. "This is a lesson every son needs to learn," his father had said. "Who you can truly trust. She was a whore and not worth your time, a girl but to fuck and chuck. Don't be angry with me, son. If she had declined my advances, she would've been the one for you. But all commoners are trouble. Money grubbing sluts. It's why we don't mix with them."

Brian didn't care what the man had said and informed his mother about what he'd seen and what his father had told him. His mother's response: "Men will be men, Brian dear. They need their flings. And if you ask me, he did you a favor. I never liked that girl."

After that, Brian had lost all faith in love, in true relationships. In his world, there was no such thing. No room for it. Love was a poor-to-working-class person's thing. The movies, where couples wound up together despite terrible odds and lived happily ever after—which such films were made by rich people—were designed to keep the commoner filled with false hope.

As soon as Daphne, wearing candy-apple red pumps, stumbled into his apartment, she stopped abruptly and said, "Holy shit."

Brian smiled, hooked his arm around hers and said, "C'mon, I'll give you the tour." It was the usual thing he did, leading her around like a princess. How he took such pleasure in seeing a woman's eyes light up, her shock at what could be if she landed him—for he knew what they were thinking. The bedroom was always the second to last place he went before heading back to the spacious living room. He needed his prey to feel secure. Safe. To see that he wasn't only interested in one thing. There was more to him. The living room was pressureless, welcoming, and said that he had no preconceived notions.

"Do you have anything to drink?" Daphne asked, curling a finger around a lock of golden blonde hair.

"What's your poison?" he asked, thinking she didn't need another, but if that's what it took, then so be it. How she had been able to down so many Cosmos and Fireballs and then eat two hot dogs as they made their way to the car, he didn't know.

"Vodka," she said and pumped her fist in the air as she whipped back her head. "I love vodka." She lost her balance and stumbled backward onto his plush recliner. Her legs came up and opened wide, causing her red mini skirt to ride up and reveal a pink-pantied crotch. "Whoops," she said, and covered her plump red lips with a well-manicured hand.

Damn, he thought. *I can't wait to have those beauties wrapped around my cock.*

He was going to have to be careful with her. Not allow her to get much drunker. He was worried she was a lush, one of those women who went out, blacked out, and had no clue what had happened. Just a party girl who didn't give a shit. Fucking a passed out woman was not his thing either, he wanted her awake and able to remember the evening. He was a bastard with morals.

"Be right back," he said and headed over to the other side of the room where a bar waited. He went behind it. "Vodka and . . . ?"

"Surprise me," she said and kicked off her heels.

Pleased by her actions, he grinned as he brought

out a glass, orange juice from the fridge, and vodka. He made a weak Screwdriver and carried it over to her.

"Thank you," Daphne said with a huge smile, showing off her incredibly straight teeth. She then brought the glass to her luscious lips and downed the beverage in two gulps before holding the empty glass out for Brian to take.

He eyed her, tilting his head.

She continued to smile and ran her tongue across her top row of teeth.

"You drank that kind of fast," he said and went to take the glass from her when she pulled it away. His eyes remained locked onto hers. She was a frisky one.

"How about a trade?" she asked.

"What do you propose?" he asked, intrigued.

"This glass for your pants."

He bit his lower lip. So she wanted to take charge. He could let her, at least in the beginning.

"Deal," he said, and this time when he reached for the glass, she let him take it. Turning around, he placed it on a coaster that was on the glass coffee table. As he did this, he felt a tug on his pants. He turned back around to see Daphne sitting on the edge of the cushion, legs spread and skirt hiked way up. There were those pink panties again.

She worked at his belt, unbuckling it in seconds. She undid the button and then slid down the zipper. His pants fell around his ankles, revealing his navy blue boxers.

Brian stood still, waiting with eagerness to see what she was going to do next. Tease? Play around? Or go for it? At this rate, it didn't matter. Daphne wasn't going to be a challenge.

"What have we here?" she asked, staring at the bulge in his boxers. He was semi- hard already.

"Up to you to find out," he said.

"Let's see . . . " She rubbed her right hand over the tented area, then curled her fingers into the waistband and slowly pulled down the boxers. His penis came free when the elastic waistband passed the head, popping out like a curious creature whose home was destroyed.

Daphne's eyes widened at the sight. "Someone's been feeding this thing."

She leaned in and he felt her hot breath on his tender flesh. A wave of ecstasy fell over him. His cock continued to fill with blood, further hardening it. His focus was on her lips and how fucking inviting they were.

She drew to within a half inch of the head and flicked her tongue at it. He spasmed with pleasure. She licked the tip and sent another shudder of pleasure to his balls. His cock grew harder still, its size almost menacing.

"Oh my," Daphne said. "This is going to be a challenge." She placed her hands on his hips, slid onto her knees and waddled in a circle, turning him around. With his back to the chair now, she gave him a shove.

Brian fell onto the recliner, and before he knew it, Daphne was slipping his shoes and socks off, then his pants and boxers. She flung them over her shoulder and hiccupped. "Oops," she said, covering her mouth and stifling a giggle.

Brian wanted her lips on his throbbing cock. The woman was more than his normal pickup. She had a vibe to her, energy. She was different. There was something in her eyes. A sly power, as if she was more than she appeared, but obviously a total slut.

Daphne clenched his outer thighs and scooted forward. She leaned in, her breath caressing his penis. "I don't normally do this sort of thing. Well, not this quickly." She winked at him, then opened her mouth and enveloped him.

She was a professional, like the fluffer on a porn set. It took all he had not to blow his load when she took in his whole girth, licking his balls with her tongue. But he was a pro too, and in no way was he going to come yet. Not that he couldn't recharge and fuck her in twenty minutes, maybe sooner, but why do that when he didn't need to.

But she was good. Really good. Even great. Strong, warm, and used her mouth muscles in ways he'd never experienced. But at the same time, she was gentle, moving slowly and using her tongue to drive him wild. She sped up, then slowed down, only to repeat the process. She must've known when he was close to coming, because she'd let up just enough so he calmed.

After five minutes of the most intense blowjob he'd ever had, he realized there was no way he was going to be able not to come. He wanted to stop her, regain his composure, but the ecstasy was too great. He didn't care—wanted to fill her mouth with his seed. She'd be into it, he knew.

As he neared climax, his eyes closed, the warmth of her mouth vanished. He waited a moment, feeling only the cool air of his air-conditioned apartment. Opening his eyes, he saw her sitting back, her face white as a sheet. She blinked hard and burped.

"Oh, God," she said. "I think I might've drunk too much."

Nooooooo," he thought. *This isn't happening.*

"You'll be fine," he said. "Just keep going. I was just about to come. Then I'll take care of you."

She looked at him, eyebrows bunching together. "No, I think I need to—"

"No," Brian said, a little too forcefully and sat up. "Please, it was so good. Just finish me off, then I'll eat you out until you come five times. Please." He couldn't believe he was begging. It was pathetic. What the hell was wrong with him?

Daphne shook her head and went to get up. Brian grabbed her by the sides of her head and pulled her to his groin. Her arms shot out and pressed against his stomach.

"Shit, girl, I'll be quick. I promise." Her lips were inches from the tip of his pre-come leaking penis. A few sucks and he'd blow.

Then. It. Happened.

The woman's mouth and eyes opened wide. A bear-like growl emitted from her, and then a stream of chunky vomit shot forth. Brian's crotch was splashed with a hot, pea soup-like substance, his neatly trimmed pubic region gone. He identified pieces of hotdog, everything else melted bits of food. His erection died, deflating like a balloon being let go to sail across a room. His sexual desire was replaced by rage. The best blowjob of his life had become his worst. He'd be scarred forever, maybe unable to ever be blown again without the fear of being vomited on.

"You fucking bitch," he hollered and sat forward, throwing the woman off him. She flew backward, arms flailing wildly as she tried to catch herself. Vomit laced spittle spattered from her lips and chin. She hit the coffee table and stopped cold, a dull thud sounding. Her eyes widened upon impact, but only for a second before the lids relaxed. He saw the light go out in them, her baby blues fading. She slumped to the floor and lay in a crumpled heap, legs bent awkwardly beneath her.

Brian stared at her face as a wave of panic rose within him. Her unblinking eyes and distant stare told him the story. There was a pulpy mat of pink flesh, hair, and blood on the corner of the table where her head had collided with it. A pool of crimson was forming around her head, spreading out like poured strawberry syrup.

"Fuck," he whispered, and then hurled as the stench of the vomit on his lap combined with what he'd done hit him. He decorated the corpse's pelvic region with what looked like oatmeal made with too much water.

Finished, he took a moment to gather his wits, and then shot out of the chair. He kneeled next to the body and placed his index and middle finger to the side of its throat.

No pulse.

Shit, he couldn't give up on her.

Using his hand, he wiped away the puke from her mouth and put his lips to hers. He attempted to perform mouth-to-mouth resuscitation, but wound up gagging. Even though he'd just vomited, he was somehow able to taste her vomit, and it made him nauseous again. He hurled once more and plastered the corpse's face in muck. Panicked, he cleared away her mouth and again attempted to revive her. This time he was able to force air into her lungs without puking. But he wasn't able to bring her back from the dead. He tried chest compressions next, but to no avail. Blood was still gushing from her scalp, her blonde hair glistening with crimson. He lifted her head and saw the wound, a nasty, skull-deep gouge.

That was it. She wasn't coming back.

CHAPTER 2

EVEN WITH ALL his money and multitude of contacts there was nothing Brian could do to fix what had been done. He'd killed someone. Well, it had been an accident. It wasn't like he'd planned it, or had malicious intentions. It was an accident, if there ever was such a thing. But how would the authorities view it? The media?

Maybe Daphne had come from a wealthy family. A family that had connections. He didn't think that was the case, but he couldn't be sure. Most likely she was a nobody. Had parents that had disowned her long ago or simply didn't give a shit about her and could care less that she was dead. However, seeing that he was rich, they'd get some douchebag lawyer who was looking for publicity and bring a shitload of trouble to his door.

He supposed he could call some people he knew, individuals who knew individuals who dealt with situations like his. But then his secret would be out. His friend, Dell, a cold-hearted prick, knew the right people, had associates who dealt with and cleaned up messes.

Brian didn't like the idea though. He'd always taken care of his shit on his own. Relying on others was weak. The more people that got involved the more likely down the road when one of them was busted for something—DWI or murder—they would talk. Spill the beans on their past and all the people they had helped.

He could call the cops, tell them she was drunk and slipped on her own puke. He'd have to reposition the body maybe and smear vomit on her heels. It could work. Or would it? Technology today was incredible. The coroner might be able to tell how she died, the force of the impact and everything. Blood flow and how it streaked her scalp and spread around the body.

Shit. There were simply too many unknowns. As of now, no one knew what had happened. The best thing for him to do was to clean it up by himself.

But how?

He could chop her up and throw the pieces into the ocean. Or melt her with acid in the bathtub. Or carry her out in a rolled up rug.

Thinking on it, Brian thought the latter of the three options was the best and least messy. He didn't think he would have the stomach to mutilate a corpse in any way. He could use the service elevator to avoid the doorman seeing him. Though Serge had some of the best kept secrets around, if he saw Brian carrying out a rug on his shoulder to a car, suspicion would be high. If an investigation ever found its way to his front door, his little late night rug disposal would shine a spotlight on his guilt.

So it was settled. He was going to carry the body out in a rolled up rug, using the service elevator. But first, he needed to clean himself up.

***

Twenty minutes passed since deciding how he was going to dispose of the body, Brian stood in his living room, showered and dressed in clean sweatpants, a T-shirt, and sneakers. Everything he'd been wearing, puke covered or not, had been placed in a garbage bag, the bag now waiting for him at the front door.

Next, he grabbed the industrial strength shop-vac from the maintenance closet—not having used such a thing since he was a boy—and sucked up all the puke and blood on the body and around it. He then grabbed the two bottles of bleach he kept under the sink and doused the body and the area around it before sucking it all up with the vacuum. He then poured bleach into the machine's nozzle. Bleach was supposed to be an evidence killer, so he figured use it everywhere. If caught, the vacuum would be filled with useless material.

Heading into his bedroom, he rolled up the $500,000 Oriental rug that he'd ordered from Milan and carried it out to the living room. *Fuck*, Brian thought. It was about to cost him half a million dollars to dispose of a body. He couldn't do it, and wondered why he hadn't thought of that until now. The rug in his den was about the same size, but had only cost him $200,000. Dragging the $500,000 rug back to his bedroom, he went to the den and grabbed the less expensive rug. For a moment, he wondered if cutting up the body and carrying it out in plastic bags was the better option. But only for a moment. Throwing away $200,000 was acceptable.

CHAPTER 3

HENRIETTA WAS SOUND asleep in her four-poster bed when she bolted upright, a horrible feeling of dread weighing her down. Though having no memory of a nightmare, she originally believed it was the reason for her abrupt waking, but when the hollow despair filling her gut didn't dwindle, she knew something bad had happened to her daughter.

Glancing at the alarm clock on the nightstand, she saw that the time was 3:15 a.m. Daphne should be sound asleep. She knew her daughter had a wild side, loved to party, but this surely had to be a mistake. She'd talked with her and they'd agreed she would quiet down with her wild ways.

Hopping out of bed, she hurried over to her mirror of scrying and spoke the magical words that would allow her to see her daughter. The mirror's surface didn't waver, indicating there was nothing to see.

Henrietta's stomach tightened. Worry gripped her chest. She sucked in a deep, steadying breath before looking into the mirror and repeating the magical words. She waited, her fingers rubbing together. When the mirror didn't react, she wondered if it was broken. Maybe time for a replacement?

Forcing a smile—because remaining positive was always key—she spoke the spell of scrying again, but this time used the name Puff Puff. To her dismay, the mirror's surface wavered and the image of her black cat resting on the kitchen windowsill came into view, dazzling moonlight glinting off her sheen fur.

Henrietta killed the spell by waving a shaky hand in front of her. Her breathing grew shallower. If the mirror was working properly, then it meant Daphne was—No. She couldn't think it. Something had to be wrong with the mirror. Or maybe her daughter had put up a blocking spell to keep her mother from spying on her. If Daphne was having sex at that very moment, it would explain things.

Or would it?

Henrietta's motherly intuition alarm was going off. Her stomach was still in knots. Being a much more powerful witch than her daughter, she could break Daphne's blocking spell should the young lady have used one. Spy on her daughter and draw her wrath. But Daphne did deserve her privacy.

Henrietta headed back to bed, trying to convince herself that her daughter was fine and that the hollowness she was experiencing was indigestion. Maybe the Eye of Newt soup hadn't been cooked enough before she ate it.

Ten minutes later, unable to sleep and realizing a bad batch of Eye of Newt soup led to hallucinations, not hollowness and despair, she sprang out of bed again and sat in front of the scrying mirror. Opening the drawer of the desk the mirror sat on, she pulled out a small ornate glass bottle and downed a hint of the Toe of Frog and Peacock Feather potion inside. She then performed the incantation that would break a blocking spell and found there was nothing to break. Sadly, she knew this could only mean one thing.

Daphne was dead.

***

After bawling, giving in to her emotions to get them out of the way, she changed into her nighttime flying stealth mode dress. The midnight purple garment was imbued with powerful cloaking enchantments, making her virtually invisible to normal human eyes. Ready for the next step in dealing with her daughter's death, Henrietta grabbed her broom, flew up the chimney and into the warm night air.

Her travels took her from West Babylon on Long Island to Manhattan, where she knew her daughter lived and liked to party. Hovering over the Empire State Building, Henrietta withdrew a pouch containing Turtle Shell dust and sprinkled it in the air as she spoke a spell that would allow her to locate her daughter's body.

CHAPTER 4

BRIAN HEFTED THE RUG—held closed with duct tape—containing the dead woman onto his shoulder and carried it out of his apartment to the service elevator. He traveled down to the parking garage where his Mercedes waited in his assigned parking space and over to the vehicle. He hadn't stopped to rest once, wanting to get the body out of his hands as soon as possible. And even though he was a large man who worked out regularly, the task at hand was taxing. His arm and leg muscles ached and his T-shirt was plastered to his flesh, soaked with sweat.

Standing at the rear of his car, shoulder achy, he reached into his pocket and withdrew the Mercedes' remote and hit the *open trunk* button. He leaned over and let the rug with the body in it fall into the almost vacant space. It landed with a dull thud, the car bouncing from the item's weight. One end of the rug stuck out, the end with her feet, if he remembered correctly. With little effort, he pushed and bent the rug, easily making it fit inside.

With the task half completed, he closed the trunk, climbed behind the steering wheel, and drove away.

Next stop: a gas station.

CHAPTER 5

HENRIETTA COULDN'T BELIEVE her little girl was gone. As much as she tried keeping her emotions in check, they kept rearing their ugliness. Her mind and soul were on a roller coaster, feelings of sadness quickly replaced by rage only to find the sadness return. They swirled about each other like two fighting tigers.

After performing the locator spell, she followed the golden trail—that only she could see—to a Mercedes traveling along the West Side Highway. Even though no human eye could see her, she didn't need any otherworldly eyes on her and remained a good hundred feet above the vehicle. When it disappeared into the Brooklyn Battery Tunnel, she met it on the other side, flying over the Hudson River. She then tailed the overly expensive car to a deserted warehouse area along the river. She watched a man exit the car and heft a rolled up rug out of the trunk, the object seeming to weigh more than it should. And she knew why as soon as she saw that the golden locator trail led directly to the rug.

Henrietta's breath hitched in her chest as her jaw quivered. She hadn't thought her baby had died of natural causes, but now it was confirmed. She'd been murdered, and now the man responsible was going to throw her away like trash. It wasn't enough that he'd killed her.

Henrietta gritted her teeth, knuckles turning white as she squeezed the broom handle. She'd seen enough, it was time to—

The man had released the rug, leaving it next to the dumpster, and was heading back to the car. Curious, Henrietta watched as the killer took two red gasoline cans from the backseat.

He was going to burn her! Burn her little girl's body!

Henrietta tilted the tip of her broom toward the ground and raced to the asphalt. She landed like a bird on a wire. Without a sound, she flipped the broom around and held it in her hands like a baseball bat. Creeping up behind the man, she raised the broom over her head and brought it down as hard as she could on the back of the man's skull.

CHAPTER 6

BRIAN WOKE ON a cold cement floor. His back was stiff, but it was the aching in his head that bothered him. Sitting up, he groaned as the throbbing increased within his skull, the flow of blood changing.

Wincing, he looked around.

He was in what appeared to be a windowless basement of some kind. Two light bulbs with pull strings hung from the ceiling. White, unmarked cinderblock walls surrounded him. To his right, against the far wall, was a washer and dryer, both items appearing like they'd been around since the 1950s, but in pristine condition as if they had never been used. Gray, metal shelves teeming with cardboard boxes stood adjacent to the clothes-cleaning machines.

To Brian's left was a staircase leading up. Beyond the staircase was inky darkness. He didn't understand how the room's light didn't penetrate that area, as if it was a black void of nothingness. He thought he saw movement on the floor, just inside the darkness.

"Hello?" he called out as he stood. The clink of a chain surprised him, causing him to look down at his feet. His ankle was manacled, a chain leading to a steel plate bolted to the wall. Panic seized him. He gripped the chain and pulled. Nothing gave. The lock keeping the manacle around his ankle had no combination or key hole.

He thought for a moment, wondering how he wound up where he was. The last thing he remembered was— He swallowed, feeling like there was a walnut lodged in his throat. The dead woman! He'd been getting the gasoline he'd purchased on the way to the warehouse district out of the backseat and then WHAM! White hot pain and bright light sparked across his vision. Now he was in a basement. Someone had clobbered him. Then what, taken him captive? He felt his head, where the pain seemed to be radiating from, and came across a nasty gash.

Movement from the darkness caught his attention.

"Hello?" he said.

No answer.

He called out again, louder this time, but heard no reply and saw no movement. He must have imagined seeing something.

Whoever had abducted him either wasn't home or was ignoring him. Rest assured, he guessed his kidnapper hadn't called the police. He or she wanted him for themselves. For what reason, he didn't know. Before he worried about it, he was going to see what was wanted of him.

Deciding it best to stay calm and reserve his energy, he sat back and leaned against the wall. Whatever was going on, he'd be ready for it.

***

With no reference of time, time itself seemed to crawl. In fact, it seemed non-existent. There were no sounds except for his breathing, the scraping of his manacle and the clink of the chain as he adjusted himself.

After a while—how long he had no idea—the rush of blood in his ears and the beating of his heart became intolerable. A constant in the absolute quiet. He cleared his throat, hummed and even spoke to himself to keep from losing his cool. It was difficult not wondering what he was doing there. Did his captor leave him there to die? Starve? Was he being watched? Recorded?

He was getting ahead of himself. For surely he'd only been in the basement for a few hours. The place was clean too, which meant it was kept up. Visited regularly. There was no crud on the floor, no cobwebs along the ceiling and no odor of mildew.

As time continued to pass like thick molasses down a rocky hill, Brian grew antsier and antsier, to the point he was pacing in the small amount of space the chain slack permitted. Unable to wait, he called out, asking for someone to talk to him, and when that didn't work, he called for help until his throat went dry, then hoarse.

Eventually, as impossible as it had seemed a few hours ago, weariness fell over him and he nodded off.

***

Brian awoke to a tickling sensation on his ankle. He reached down to scratch the itch when he saw a giant gray rat sink its teeth into his flesh. "Oooowwww," he cried in both pain and shock, then kicked at the beady-eyed rodent. The creature squeaked as it skidded away. Brian checked his ankle and saw blood trickling from the bite mark.

"Shit," he said and squeezed the skin around the wound, forcing it to bleed more. "You have to get the disease out," his mother had told him when he was eight-years old and had been scratched by a rusty nail poking through his aunt's porch.

Looking up, he saw the rat a few feet away. It was sitting up and looking at him. "Shoo," he said and waved his arm at it.

"Fuck you," the rat said, its voice screechy.

Brian's jaw fell as he stared at the thing, his fingers no longer having the strength to squeeze his flesh.

The rat stood on its hind legs. "I'm hungry too, you know. No need to be so rude."

Brian looked around, expecting to see someone, a human someone. "Okay, asshole. Enough of this shit. Show yourself."

"I'm right here, moron," the rat said, hands on its hips.

Brian stared at the creature, jaw slack. He closed his eyes and said aloud, "I'm imagining this. My mind has cracked."

"Your mind's cracked all right, moron," the rat said.

Shit, Brian thought. Not seeing it wasn't helping. He opened his eyes.

The rat shook its head and said, "Ah, to be new again."

"New?"

"A new arrival," the rat said. "Was so long ago when I first arrived."

Brian couldn't believe he was talking to a rat. If his leg wasn't smarting from the bite, he would have assumed he was dreaming.

"I'm sorry about the bite, but it's what I do. Who I am, you know?"

Brian opened his mouth to speak, but found no words.

A door opened at the top of the stairs.

The rat straightened. "Time for me to scram," it said and scurried into the darkness.

Brian wanted to call out after it, but told himself he was going to forget all about the last few minutes, chalking it up to hysteria.

Pink slippered feet landed on the top step and soon the figure was descending. She wore a flower embroidered dress with frilly sleeves that opened at the wrists like bellbottom jeans. Her hair was cotton white and extended past her shoulders. Brian guessed she was around seventy-years old, give or take, basing his assumption on the slightly wrinkled flesh around her blue eyes.

He hadn't been sure what to expect—maybe a muscled, tattooed, intimidating fellow, or someone wearing dark sunglasses, with slicked back hair who would speak with a foreign accent—but an elderly woman? What was she, the mother of a group of backwoods psychopaths? Based on the cleanliness of the place, he doubted that was the case.

"Good, you're awake," she said, reaching the floor and making her way over to him.

"What do you want?" he asked, figuring he'd get right to the point.

"I've got him," she said, smiling, but there was no humor in her eyes. The woman wasn't some sweet old grandma, but something wicked.

"Got who?" he asked. "Because I think you've got me con—"

"—fused with someone else?" she asked, finishing his sentence.

He looked at her, inhaled a steadying gulp of air, then said, "Look, I've obviously been kept alive for a reason. Tell your boss if he wants to talk to come down here and do so himself."

The woman's smile vanished and her eyes bore in on him.

"You little shit," she said. "You pig-headed bastard. You think I'm someone to trifle with?"

Brian felt his will dwindling under her gaze, but he held his own and stared back. He couldn't look away—needed this old hag to know he wasn't afraid.

"Lady," he finally said, breaking the silence between them, "go get the man in charge and stop wasting my time."

The woman's cheeks reddened. She looked ready to explode. But a moment later her face softened and she smiled. "Thirsty?" she asked.

"A glass of water would be appreciated."

"I'm sure it would." The woman turned and headed back up the stairs.

Brian wasn't sure pissing off his kidnapper's mother—if that's who she was—was a good idea, but he wasn't about to let the old hag have any satisfaction.

He waited for her return. Time moved excruciatingly slow again. When she didn't come back, he hoped the man in charge was on his way to see him. But after a while, he lost hope of anything. He was left alone again. With no reason not to, except for his parched throat, he yelled for someone to talk to him. To work out whatever it was they wanted. Negotiate his release.

As time went by, hunger heated up his gut. He found it surprising that he had an appetite and began wondering how long he'd been there. It couldn't have been more than five hours. But truth be told, he really had no fucking clue.

A pair of red glowing eyes suddenly shone from the darkness beyond the stairs. "Psst," a voice said. "You'd be best not to piss off the old bat."

Oh, great, he thought, *I'm hearing the rat again.*

He wasn't going to give in to his delusions again. Maybe his captor had drugged him, kept him asleep for days—hence his famished feeling—and that's why he was hallucinating.

The red eyes vanished.

There, you see, he told himself. *Ignore the bullshit my mind conjures and I can keep myself sane.*

Sitting back, allowing time to roll by—though it really crawled—his strength waned. He was starving and the only thing to counter the hunger pangs was to sleep.

He lay down, closed his eyes and dozed on the uncomfortably hard cement floor.

CHAPTER 7

BRIAN AWOKE TO a sharp, biting pain on his right hand. He looked to see the gray rat gnawing on the plump flesh between his thumb and forefinger. Instead of jerking his hand away, he grabbed the furry rodent around its waist and got to his feet. The disease-carrying creature squealed like a pig as it kicked its legs.

"Please don't kill me," the rat begged, its scrawny hands clamped together in prayer.

Disgusted, Brian rose to his feet, surprised the critter wasn't biting and clawing him. Without hesitating, he threw the rat to the ground as hard as he could, and before it could get up, crushed it beneath his sneakers. The rat's screams were cut short as its insides were mushed and its bones crushed. Blood and guts exploded from its mouth and eyes, one of them popping completely out and bouncing a few feet away.

"Got you, you little—"

Brian couldn't believe what he'd done and what he was doing. Not only had he killed a rat by crushing it to death, but he was talking to its corpse. He wondered if it was there at all. His hand throbbed and it was bleeding, crimson droplets dotting the floor.

Whatever was happening, he decided right then and there that the rat was real, just like his wound, but the rodent had not spoken. That part had been in his head.

He kicked the rat corpse, sending it across the room—portions of its insides spilling out—where it hit the wall and flopped to the floor. Lifting his leg, he saw that the bottom and sides of his sneaker were caked in gore. He flicked his sneaker, getting the larger pieces of meat and hair off the footwear.

Shaken, but not having realized it until now, his knees buckled, but he did not fall. He was ravished with hunger, his stomach filled with needles. He grew angry at how he was being treated and yelled, "You can't just fucking leave me down here. Tell me what you want."

Brian knew what he wanted—his freedom. But for now, he'd take food. Anything, even a sardine sandwich, and he despised sardines. He thought about begging for food, giving his captors what they wanted, if that's what they wanted. But he held his tongue for now.

Realizing he was going to get no response, he rubbed a hand over his face and felt a thick growth of hair. Not understanding, he rubbed his jaw and lips, feeling a bushel of hair. He had a beard. How the hell could that be? He'd been clean shaven every day since he had started growing facial hair. How long had he been locked up?

A cold sweat broke out across his skin, the flesh rippling. He rubbed his hand through his hair and felt its thickness and length, the growth past his ears. His heart was racing, the powerful muscle sent into overdrive. He couldn't understand the hair, how it was possible, unless he'd been held captive for a good length of time. Six months? A year?

As he stood there, trembling, his eyes focused on the dead rat and the impossible sight before him. The rat's corpse was moving, as if teeming with maggots. The blood and guts splayed across the floor were moving too, traveling toward the rat. Its eye rolled back to the socket and popped itself back in. Blood and guts poured back into the rat's mouth. The whole scene was like watching a reversed time-lapse video. The rat's corpse inflated as more excretions filled it. In moments, it was normal-looking again. The creature coughed, and then its red eyes came to life as it sat up, yawned and stretched as if waking from a deep, restful sleep. It pushed itself up and stood. "I hate when that happens."

Brian screamed and grabbed the sides of his head. He fell to his knees and yelled, "Get the fuck away from me, devil."

The rat stopped moving. It pointed a finger at itself. "Me, a devil?" It laughed, keeling over and hugging its belly. "I wish."

"What's wrong with me?" Brian asked aloud. He looked at his shaking hands. He couldn't believe what he'd said. Devil? He didn't believe in such things. What was he, a Pilgrim straight off the Mayflower?

The air seemed too thick to breathe. He pawed at his shirt collar, trying to stretch it out so he could get oxygen. The room spun and his vision was clouding. Trying to blink away the fog, the room started tilting.

Brian crashed to the floor, the hit hard and jarring. He screamed again, begging for the nightmare he was caught in to end. Tears streaked his cheeks, eyes red.

He sobbed for a while, and like a crying child, tired himself out. He lay there, tear-streaked and drool covered. Quiet.

"I wouldn't keep doing that, my friend," the squeaky rat's voice said.

Brian sat up and wiped his face using his forearm. If he was in some kind of hell—maybe *the* Hell, then he was going to make the best of it.

Not seeing the rat anywhere, he assumed it was in the darkness. Staring into the void, he said, "Do what?"

"Sleep," the rodent said. "I wouldn't do that if I didn't absolutely have to."

"And why not?"

"Can't say. The missus would skin me again. Make it so my fur didn't grow back for a year. Do you know how cold it gets in the winter?"

"Whatever," Brian said, waving a hand dismissively.

"Seriously, man," the rat said. "Stay awake for as long as you can. You'll thank me later."

Not wanting to let it go, Brian again asked why he shouldn't sleep. When the rat didn't answer, he asked again. Hearing no reply, he assumed the creature had left, gone off to wherever it had come from.

However, something in the creature's voice rang true, and he decided he would do everything in his power not to sleep. Right now, he wasn't tired. He hadn't been tired when he'd slept before either. Had only done so because he wanted the escape.

But he was thirsty beyond belief.

And hungry.

Getting to his feet, he shook out his arms and legs, rolled his neck and rotated his hips. He felt better already, much more alert.

The door at the top of the stairs opened. Brian took a step back toward the wall, somewhat anxious.

The person coming down the stairs came into view. It was the elderly lady again. This time her white hair was neatly up in a bun. She wore a dark purple dress with a yellow sickle moon on the front. She was holding a tray with a glass filled with a clear liquid that he supposed was water, and a wooden bowl.

She came over to him. "Good, you're awake."

"How long have I been here?"

The woman laughed. "Suddenly you care? Not all business anymore?"

"If you want something from me, you're going to have to keep me alive."

"Staying alive is completely up to you, Mr. James." She stepped to him and placed the tray on the floor before stepping back. He could've grabbed her. Threatened to kill her if she didn't let him go. But he couldn't kill her or he might never be able to leave, and the fact that she showed no fear of him was alarming.

Brian's eyes bulged from their sockets. The liquid in the glass had to be water. If it was something like bleach or some other chemical he would've smelled it. The bowl looked like it contained some kind of soup, maybe chicken.

"Go ahead," Mr. James," the woman said. "Drink. Eat."

He looked at her. Then at the glass. Then back at the woman.

"It's not poisoned, I promise."

Keeping his sights on the woman, he reached down and picked up the glass. It was cold, the frigidness invigorating and almost painful. He brought the glass to his nose and sniffed. Still not detecting an odor but for the odor of water, he took a sip. His pallet exploded with glory, his salivary ducts working again. He'd never tasted anything so delicious. It was the purity of the water, he knew. Amazed at how the common substance could provide such euphoria.

Not wanting to waste another moment, he started downing the water, gulping it, and nearly choked.

"Easy, Mr. James," the woman said.

He cleared his throat and continued to swallow the wonderful fluid, the fluid he'd taken for granted and hardly consumed. As he chugged, he told himself that he would never take it for granted again.

When he was finished—the glass with merely a few droplets in it—his stomach felt as if a beach ball had been inflated in it. "Thank you," he said and placed the glass back on the tray. Though feeling like he had no room in his belly, he picked up the bowl of soup, and upon closer examination, saw that it was indeed chicken noodle soup.

Holding the warm bowl in the one hand, he held the spoon in the other and began eating. The woman stood before him, watching. Her arms were crossed over her chest. Brian didn't care what she was doing. She could stare at him all day if it meant he could eat and drink.

When he was finished, he returned the bowl to the tray. Upon standing, he let loose a cheek flapping burp and made a little more room in his stomach.

Saying nothing, the woman picked up the tray and headed back upstairs.

"Wait," Brian said. "Aren't you going to tell me what this is about? What you want from me?"

She disappeared up the stairs, only to return to the basement a few minutes later, holding a bucket. She placed it in front of him.

"What's this for?" he asked, believing it was to be his toilet.

"You're going to need it soon," she said.

He shook his head. "I'm supposed to relieve myself in a damn pail?"

"That's entirely up to you, but if I were you, I wouldn't." She turned and headed back up the stairs.

Brian said nothing this time as she left. He was done begging for answers. He needed to spend his energy on finding a way out of his predicament. A way to escape. And as hard as it was to believe he was doing it, he called out to the rat.

"Yes?" the squeaky voice asked from somewhere in the darkness.

"Can you help me get out of here?"

"No."

"Why not?"

"Because it's not in my nature to help. I'm a rat and must do what rats do."

"Well, rats don't talk and you do that," Brian said.

"This is true," the rat said. "But I'm still a rat."

"You're afraid of the lady," Brian said. "That's why you won't help me."

"Also true," the rat said.

He should've known the rat—for surely it wasn't real—wouldn't be able to help. It was after all only a figment of his imagination, at least the talking part.

"How about an idea on how I could get out of here?" Brian asked.

"Do what the witch asks and you'll get out of here, but it won't be easy."

Witch? he thought. He didn't believe in such things. But apparently a part of his mind did. He sat back against the wall, letting the food he'd eaten digest, when his stomach made a loud sloshing sound, followed by a gurgling. His abdominal muscles clenched. Sharp pain stabbed him and he hunched over, clutching his belly. He figured it was due to eating so much after being so hungry. The digestion pangs would cease, come and go. But the stabbing continued. He cried out as his stomach further tightened. The gurgling grew louder and more violent, shaking him. Sweat trickled down his face. The bitch had poisoned him. The onset of whatever was happening to him had been too fast for it to be normal. He groaned and rocked back and forth before falling onto his side and curling into a ball. Nausea fell over him as his flesh lost its warmth. He knew this feeling and what it meant.

Sitting up, he pulled the bucket toward him and vomited a stream of partially digested chicken soup into it. With puke-laced saliva dripping from his lower lip, he spit and breathed. To his surprise, the bucket was fuller than he thought it ought to be. Staring at the vomit, breathing in the hot fumes proved a bad idea. His stomach clutched again and he hurled. Still feeling sick, he knew he wasn't done, and a moment later, upchucked again.

After the third heave, he felt better. Weak, but more like his old self. Using his tongue, he fished around his mouth, found a few pieces of chicken and noodle and spit them into the bucket. Finished, he wiped his mouth using his forearm and pushed the receptacle away, then sat against the wall.

"That looked like it sucked," the rat said.

Brian chuckled, unable to help himself. "Looks like I've made a friend for life." He shook his head. "I'm going to need some serious therapy to get rid of you."

"Don't know about all that," the rat said, "but are you going to eat that?"

"The vomit?"

"Yes."

"No. Please, help yourself."

Red eyes appeared in the darkness. A pattering of feet sounded as the rat approached, its gray body coming into view. It came right up to the bucket, rose on its hind legs and sniffed the container's lip. "Yummy. Are you sure you don't mind?"

"By all means, have at it."

The door at the top of the stairs opened.

The rat swore and snapped its fingers, then darted back to the darkness.

"I heard you, Rat," the woman said as she descended the staircase.

"Sorry, my lady," the rat said. "But it's in my nature to eat such things."

"That's all well and good, but if you want to remain alive, you will leave Mr. James' food alone."

"Yes, my lady," the rat said.

The old woman still wore the dark purple dress with the yellow sickle moon on it. She walked up to Brian and said, "You want answers? Well, I'm going to give them to you."

CHAPTER 8

BRIAN COULDN'T BELIEVE what the old woman had told him. She was Daphne's mother, the woman who had died—accidentally—in his apartment. She was also a witch. He'd tried telling her that her daughter's death was an accident, that he didn't kill her. They had been having a great time until she slipped.

"I'm telling you, your daughter—" he began, but was cut off.

"I know exactly what happened, Mister," she shouted, and he could have sworn the walls shook. "I cast a spell that temporarily brought life back into her. Her spirit told me everything, how you took advantage of her and forced her to suck your cock even though she was sick. You ignored her and she vomited all over you and your furniture."

Stunned, having no idea how she knew what had happened, he fought through his shock and said, "Hell, she attacked me. Practically raped my ass."

"I know my daughter can be a horny little minx, but the bottom line is that you killed her."

"Then turn me over to the cops," Brian pleaded. "You can't keep me here like this. I won't tell them a thing about you. I'll confess to what happened with your daughter."

The woman's head flew back as a spine-tingling cackle erupted from her. She was mad. "And watch your high-priced attorneys turn my Daphne into a drunken, druggie whore? No way."

"So what then?" Brian asked. "You're going to keep me locked up forever?" People will look for me. I'll be missed."

The woman reached behind her back and produced a newspaper. She tossed it to him.

Brian picked it up, wondering what she wanted him to see when his eyes rested on the date. *It can't be*, he thought. "What kind of bullshit is this?" With a scowl on his face, he flung the paper away. "Do you expect me to believe I've been here for a year?"

"Doesn't matter what you believe," she said. "Here's the truth: You're here. You're mine. You'll only eat puke. Every time you fall asleep, a year will pass. It's up to you how long you remain here. If you die here."

"You can't do this you crazy bitch!"

She wagged a finger at him and said, "Now, now, Mr. James, that kind of talk isn't going to help you get out of here." Holding out her hand, she said something he didn't understand and the newspaper flew to her grasp. Then she turned and headed back upstairs.

"It's all true, you know," the rat said.

Brian was wondering if he was in a coma. It would explain a lot. Unfortunately, everything felt real, not foggy, surreal or dreamlike. His hunger and pain were true. He couldn't explain the beard and long hair. Maybe she'd glued the stuff on. He tugged at it and when it didn't come free, he pulled harder, stopping when his eyes watered from the pain.

"She really is a witch," the rat said. "And it's best you do as she says. You've really screwed up with her. Killing her daughter? Damn. You're fucked."

"I'm not eating puke," Brian said. "Mine or anyone else's."

"Suit yourself. But if you don't eat, you'll starve and die. If you die here, you'll never leave. You'll wind up like me, forever changed."

"So if I don't eat, she'll change me into a rat?" Brian asked.

"No. Well, maybe," the rat said. "I don't know what she'll do with you, or turn you into. You really, really did something bad."

"What did you do to become a rat?"

"Nothing I care to talk about right now."

"Oh, how convenient."

The rat said no more after that, leaving Brian alone.

CHAPTER 9

AS TIME PASSED—Brian unsure if it had been hours, weeks or months—he didn't sleep. He never truly grew tired, only depressed and stressed. The more he thought about his situation the more he believed everything was real, including the rat. But he couldn't eat his puke. He looked at it on occasion, the consistency remaining the same. He'd thought the top layer would harden into a piecrust-like state, but it hadn't. The smell too remained as horrid as when the puke was fresh.

***

Hunger ravished his core. A thousand razorblades were slicing up his stomach, the pain spreading to his head and limbs. Time continued its course, the unseen, untouchable constant the worst of all things. It never ended. Prolonged his suffering and brought on his hunger.

Finally, feeling death approaching, Brian accepted his fate and what he must do. He had asked the rat—who hadn't shown itself in a while—if he did as the woman asked would the nightmare end? Would she let him go? The gray varmint had said he thought so, and if not, then it would show the witch he was taking her seriously.

Barely able to lift the bucket, he brought the slop-containing bucket shakily to his lips. The stench assaulted his nostrils like invisible fists. Despite having nothing in his stomach, he gagged and set the bucket down before going into full-on dry-heaving.

His throat burned from the small amount of acid that had shot up his esophagus. As his eyes watered, he cleared his throat and swallowed. Fuck, he wasn't sure he was going to be able to do it. Maybe he should scoop out handfuls first. Or pick out the larger chunks, eat them and then quickly down the liquidy stuff. He could also pinch his nose closed to avoid tasting the vile meal. He used to do it when he was younger. He didn't like the taste of string beans and wasn't allowed to leave the dinner table until his plate was clean. So he'd hold his nose closed, put the vegetables in his mouth, chew and swallow them down with his drink.

With shaky arms, his muscles feeling as if they'd lost mass from having not eaten, he tilted the bucket so he could look inside it. He didn't see any chunks and hoped it would go down easily. Reaching inside, he picked up a kernel of corn, the item mostly shell. Releasing it, he prodded and poked around the soupy mess. Finally, he found a morsel he thought wouldn't go down so smoothly, one he could chew. Holding his nose closed, he tossed the pliable scrap into his mouth.

Despite pinching his nostrils closed, his palate flooded with a bitter, putrid taste—a mixture of vomit, chicken, and something else, something sinister. He couldn't figure out how this could be and squeezed his nose tighter. He continued to chew and the food easily crumbled between his teeth. More noxious flavor escaped and flooded his mouth, saturating his taste buds in warm, juicy fluids.

Unable to stop himself, his mind conjured up images of what he was doing, what he was eating. His stomach muscles hitched and before he knew it, his body lurched forward and he was dry-heaving. The masticated food in his mouth flew back into the bucket.

"It won't work," the rat said when Brian was finished.

"What won't work?" he asked, trying to swallow away the burning in his throat.

"Holding your nose. The witch wants you to suffer. You can guarantee she's made it so no matter what you do, you'll taste it."

Wonderful, he thought, shoulders slumping. He imagined that being physically assaulted—beaten with a bat or sliced with a knife—might be better than what he was going to endure.

He couldn't believe where he was. Though he came from money, he had worked his way up from the mailroom at his firm to partner. He'd done things to make it—lied, cheated, and stolen accounts—but everyone who was anyone did it too. There were no self-made millionaires with clean hands. If a person wanted to be honest, he or she remained poor. If he or she was lucky, he or she could maybe hit middle class.

He didn't deserve what was happening to him. When Daphne had died, it hadn't been on purpose. What would anyone have done if they'd been puked on? He simply reacted, shoving her away. It wasn't his fault she had lost her balance. If she hadn't been so drunk, she wouldn't have needed to puke and probably wouldn't have fallen when he'd shoved her. Shit, drunk people fell easily enough on their own.

"You're thinking how great you had it, right?" the rat asked.

"Yeah."

"Good. It's what you need to do in order to survive. Think about getting back to your life. Think about doing what the witch wants, and then do it. So the chum in the bucket tastes horrible, it's your chum. It's not like you're eating someone else's. Down that shit and show the old hag you mean business."

Brian took the rat's words to heart. He had so much to live for. To get back to. Money, women, and more money. Superficial—hell yeah, but that's what he wanted. He loved his money and all that it allowed him and the ultimate power it gave.

If he could get out of the witch's basement, he could come back with an army of killers and put her in the grave. No, screw that. He'd chain her up and make her eat his puke.

Feeling renewed, he picked up the bucket and brought it to his lips. The odor made his eyes water and his stomach turn. "Fuck this fucking shit," he yelled and starting downing the slop. He used the power of his mind and the thoughts of his luxurious life and how much he wanted to get back to it, including all the women left to bang. His throat burned as the acidy mixture flowed. Whenever a large piece entered his mouth, he paused for a few moments and chewed, fighting back the need to hurl.

Gulp! Gulp! Gulp! Down went the upchuck.

Before long, he was upending the bucket, the last of the drivel entering the hatch. When he was done, he slammed the bucket down in triumph and wanted to shout, "I did it. Take that you twisted old hag." But he couldn't. Couldn't even move. His stomach felt as if it had a bowling ball in it, full and heavy. A feeling of queasiness fell over him. Audible gurgling came from his gut.

"Keep it down," the rat said, encouragingly.

Brian closed his eyes and clamped a hand over his mouth.

He tried focusing on his penthouse apartment, tits and ass, but images of what he'd just eaten filled his mind. Pressure built to an overwhelming level before a rancid burp escaped his lips. Acid scorched his throat, causing him to cough. His abdomen gurgled loudly. The soupy slop—chunks of chicken, noodle, and carrot—swirled around in his stomach. A cold sweat broke out across his flesh while his face and chest grew heated.

He must've looked terrible, because the rat said, "Shit, man. Stay strong." Another rancid throw up burp shot up into the back of his throat. His eyes watered and his stomach rumbled.

"You're going to blow, man," the rat said.

Nausea rocked his core. He opened his eyes, needing to look at something concrete, real. Rocking, he rubbed his stomach and looked at the washing machines. Another burp escaped him, the fumes causing his eyes to further flood with tears, something they were doing a lot of lately. The energy felt as if it had been sapped from his body. The rat was talking again, but he couldn't make out the words. The vomit he'd ingested was killing him. A black abyss of misery swelled within. His vision was fading, a fuzzy aura appearing around his periphery. He was about to pass out.

But his body was going to protect him. As much as he wanted to keep the vomit inside and show the hag he was stronger than she thought, he couldn't.

Snatching the bucket and bringing it to his mouth, his diaphragm clutched and a stream of puke came forth. Then another and another, allowing him quick and much needed breaths in between.

When he had nothing left to give, he set the bucket down and shoved it away before slumping against the wall.

"You lasted longer than I thought you would," the rat said.

"Pay up, sewer dweller," another voice said.

Brian turned to see who the new arrival was, but there was only darkness.

"Who's there with you, Rat?" he asked.

"My friend, Spider," the rat said.

A large tarantula scurried forth from the darkness.

Brian's eyes widened. He despised arachnids, especially large ones.

The spider bowed, bringing one of its hairy legs in front of its multi-eyed face. "Hello, good sir," it said, the voice female sounding. "I've been busy, but when I received word of what the witch was up to, well, I had to see for myself what was happening."

Going with it, as unbelievable as it seemed, Brian said, "Did you place a bet on me, Rat?"

"Yes, he did," Spider said.

Rat emerged from the darkness. "It's routine around here for new arrivals. Nothing personal."

"And what did my anguish win you, Miss Spider, if I may call you Miss Spider?"

"You may," said Spider, "but just Spider is fine. And as far as what I won, well, dibs on eating you."

44

Brian stiffened and brought his legs in close.

Rat looked at Spider and the two laughed.

"Either of you come near me and I'll squash the shit out of you," Brian said, knowing their deaths wouldn't last long.

"We're not going to eat you right now," Rat said. "Only if you don't make it out of here alive. Spider gets first pick from your parts."

Brian shivered at the thought of the arachnid crawling over his skin and sinking her fangs into him. He didn't want Rat eating him either, but there was something far more disgusting about having Spider devour him. But he felt a little better knowing he wasn't going to have to fend off his new friends.

"Well, I am getting out of here," he said. "So betting on me is pointless."

"We said the same thing," Spider said. "And here we are."

"Yup," Rat said.

"Were you both human once?" Brian asked.

"Yes," Spider said.

"So, what happened?" Brian asked, curious.

"Our situation was different than yours," Spider said. "Rat and I were part of a witch's coven. Long story really short: we went against the majority and killed a few of our former brethren."

"Death would've been too good for us," Rat said, "so our bodies were taken and we were given these."

"Are there more of you?" Brian asked.

"Frog is out by the pond, sitting on a lily pad," Spider said. "He likes the sun and catching flies. The basement doesn't suit him. Our friend, Bat, went batty, as they say, and stays in the belfry."

The door at the top of the stairs opened. Brian's

eyes shot to the staircase. When he glanced back to where Spider and Rat had been, they were gone.

High-heeled black shoes clomped down the wooden steps. It was the witch, this time wearing a purple dress with some kind of strange runes on it. She was followed by another woman, this one wearing denim overalls. She had a long, crooked nose. A huge wart stood on the end of it.

Three more females came down the stairs, one younger, maybe in her twenties, while the others looked to be in their forties. One had frizzy orange hair. The other, pin-straight, jet-black. They were all rather pretty.

Soon, the five women stood semi-circle in front of him.

Brian remained seated.

"He did it, Henrietta," Wartnose said. "You were right."

"I had my doubts too," the forty-something one with bright orange hair said.

"It only took him two years," Henrietta said.

Two years? Brian thought. *Nice try, ladies.* He looked from one woman to the next, each one's stare intimidating. It felt as if they were studying prey, sizing him up for . . . A meal? Were they going to stick him in a pot and cook him? Or were they going to turn him into a toad or some other small creature?

"Aww, he's shaking," the young one said.

"Enough talk, ladies," Henrietta said. "We came to do a job, so let's be done with it."

Brian stared at the old hag, the apparent leader. He got to his feet. If he was going to die or be turned into something, he wasn't going to give her or the others the satisfaction of his looking scared.

46

With a wave of her wand, the puke bucket rose in the air and hovered over Brian's head. He looked up at the bottom of the container. He then watched what he'd expected to happen. The bucket tilted at a steady, slow pace.

Not wanting to get the slop in his eyes, he closed them and looked down. The warm sludge collided with the top of his head, splattering all around and over him. It dripped down his face, over his ears and along his neck and back. It leaked under his T-shirt and over it. The vomit-slide seemed to continue well past what was in the bucket, the stench wretched.

Finally, after what seemed like a barrel-full had been dumped upon him, the cascade of puke ended. Brian wiped his eyes and cleared away what he could from his face. He looked at Henrietta, glad he'd heard her name. It would make finding her when he escaped that much easier.

The bucket moved and hovered in front of the red-haired witch. Her mouth opened incredibly wide and a stream of bright green vomit shot forth. When she finished, the bucket moved to the next witch, the young one. She deposited a stomach's worth of dark tan vomit. From there, the rest of the witches took a turn, the vomit ranging from pea soup green to oatmeal tan to dark brown until the bucket was brimming with a multicolored, steaming slop.

"This is for you, Brian," Henrietta said, using his first name for a change. With the bucket still below her, she pressed a forefinger to one nostril and blew a slug-like snot from the other and sent it into the bucket. The bucket then floated to the floor in front of Brian.

"Drink up, my pretty," Henrietta said, smiling.

"You've got one day to finish it and keep it down. If you do that, I'll release you. If not, you'll never leave here. Then you can spend your time with Rat and Spider and the rest of the lot."

Brian wanted to hurl by simply looking at the bucket. He didn't know how he would be able to get it all down, but he would figure it out. "And how do I know you'll let me go after this?"

"You don't," Henrietta said, then turned and headed up the stairs. The others followed, none speaking or looking his way.

CHAPTER 10

BRIAN STARED AT the bucket, wondering how he was going to get all that puke down, let alone keep it down.

"I'd eat it little by little," Rat suggested as if reading his mind.

"Yeah," Spider said. "Take your time. Just not more than a day's worth."

"Though we wouldn't mind having another friend around here," Rat said.

"The more the merrier," Spider added.

Brian couldn't remember a time when he felt more defeated. Nothing ever got to him, not since he had discovered his father was screwing his fiancé. How something like that could have happened to him, how he couldn't have been aware of it, still haunted and baffled him to this very day. He'd closed his heart after that, having had no luck with true love. He would never be humiliated in such a way again.

Thinking about his life now and all that he'd accomplished, he wanted to cry. Not from sadness, but from sheer joy. Fuck love and relationships. He'd come to love himself. The empire, however small it was when compared to true empires, was his. All his. It was all he needed. His material possessions gave him no real trouble and left his life uncomplicated. People and relationships sucked. Sure, he had friends, but since he had been a kid, they came and went. Hanging out with people he had things in common with was fun, but he was always ready to walk away from whoever was in his life. All a person really had in life was themselves. Brian knew above all else that he could count on no one but Brian. Getting into a relationship made people weak, reliant. He couldn't allow that.

Like now, for example.

There was no one to help him but himself. No one to help him eat the puke. It was all up to him.

Feeling his spirits soar a little, despite what he had to do, he pulled the bucket close. The stench he thought he'd gotten used to worsened, causing him to gag. It was a putrid mixture of sewage, shit, rotting meat, and decaying vegetables.

Eat and hopefully be released, or die and then become one of the witch's critters. He had no choice. He had to eat.

Reaching out, he grabbed the bucket by its sides and picked it up. Its weight caught him off guard and he nearly spilled it. Settling down, his hands shaky, eyes watering, and still feeling the need to gag, he brought the bucket to his lips and drank.

The first few gulps were awful and he thought he was going to die. His body was simply going to seize up like a car engine without oil. It was a ridiculous thought, but it felt real. But through sheer determination, he kept swallowing. He needed to win, to succeed no matter what he had to go through. He was going to show the witch who was boss. He knew he couldn't possibly consume the entire bucket's contents, but he would drink until he needed to stop. When the time came, he put the bucket down and saw that it was still three fourths full. No, not full, but empty. He was usually a positive, glass-half-full person, but not today. Today, he needed the glass to be half empty.

He sat back and wiped his lips using his forearm. His stomach was full and he could smell his own rancid breath. He held his nose, but it did nothing to quell the stink. He tried gathering spit and swallowing to clean his palate, but his mouth remained vile.

As minutes ticked by, the pressure in his stomach built. It was all the air he'd taken in as he drank. Suddenly, the need to burp arrived. He fought against letting it out, fearing if he did, he'd puke up what he'd eaten. But the burn, odor, and taste would be so horrid that he wouldn't be able to stop his body from reacting.

The pressure grew. Pain, like a swarm of stinging bees, spread over his abdomen. He was a balloon ready to burst. There would be no holding the puke back, he knew. With great regret, he relaxed and let the burp go.

Scorching air shot up his throat and escaped like a rumble of thunder. The stench was paint-peeling worthy, but it was the acidy substance in his throat that made him cry out. His sinuses tingled and the room went blurry. He coughed and tried clearing his esophagus, but found no relief.

Nausea struck as he was wrapped in a blanket of sick. Reaching out, he pulled the bucket toward him. He took deep breaths, picturing his stomach as an indestructible iron chamber.

Fight it, dammit! his mind screamed.

His stomach churned and gurgled. Another throw up burp spewed up his throat, burning his tender flesh like flame. He swallowed in hopes of dousing the fire with whatever saliva he could muster.

The room spun. Breathing became difficult. His strength was sucked from him and his stomach muscles tightened. Unable to stop it, his mouth popped open and the hurling commenced. Everything he'd eaten came out, splattering the bucket and filling it again.

Exhausted and defeated, he sat back and wept, the act so foreign to him that he hadn't been sure his body was capable of such a thing. He slumped onto his side, and a few minutes later, he fell asleep.

CHAPTER 11

BRIAN AWOKE TO a stinging sensation on his right forefinger. His eyes shot open and he saw Rat nibbling on him. He jerked his hand away and sat up. "What the hell, Rat?"

Rat backpedaled and put his forelegs up defensively. Seeing he wasn't going to get grabbed, he said, "Sorry about that, but it's in my nature. I can't help myself."

"So you've told me," Brian said. "But I thought we were friends."

Rat shrugged. "We are, but I'm still a rat."

Brian shook his head. He looked around for Spider, but the eight-legged creature was nowhere to be seen.

"If you're looking for Spider," Rat said, "she's not here. She's out back with Frog. If you ask me, she uses him for food. His tongue catches everything. Makes her lazy, if you ask me."

"I thought rats ate everything too," Brian said. "Are you not hungry?"

"I'm always hungry, and we do eat almost anything. But some things are tastier than others."

As Brian continued to suck on his wounded finger, his dry, slime-coated mouth became moist with the coppery, almost sweet taste of his own blood. His salivary ducts were working again, his ability to swallow properly returned. He sucked harder on his finger, wanting more, but the wound had clotted.

Withdrawing his finger from his mouth, he eyed the wound, then the bucket of puke. Flies had come from somewhere and were sitting around the rim. Upon closer examination, he saw that they too were puking, tiny, hair-like streams of vomit coming from their suckers. The sight was as amazing as it was gross, but Brian didn't care.

"Rat," he said, "I could kiss you."

Rat's eyebrows arched high on his little forehead. "That's fine, but remember, I'm a rat."

With renewed vigor, Brian said, "I'm going to need you to keep biting me. Would that be okay?"

"Um, are you joking?" Rat asked. "I'd eat the shit out of you, literally. But c'mon, I may be a rat who can't die, but re-forming is painful."

"I won't hurt you," Brian said, assuredly. "I need your sharp teeth and my blood."

Rat agreed to bite Brian, but warned Brian that if he was tricking him and squashed him again, that the next time he fell asleep, Rat would eat one of the eyes out of his head.

Brian picked up the bucket and started drinking. His spirit was even more renewed and helped keep him from noticing the smell or taste. Well, not really, but he fought through it.

When the bucket was a quarter empty, he put it down and had Rat gnaw on his finger, creating a fresh wound. He stuck his finger in his mouth and sucked. The putrid taste filling his mouth vanished, replaced by the sweet coppery taste of his blood. He burped a few times and the stench was horrendous, but his blood kept him from feeling like he had to puke.

He gave his body time to digest the regurgitated human oatmeal before drinking again. When he was halfway done with the bucket's contents, he paused and had Rat bite him again. He flooded his mouth with blood and rested before starting on the puke again.

Brian kept at it, repeating the routine until the bucket was empty. He almost lost it a few times, nausea spreading over him like a wet blanket of sewage. But he held on and finished the meal. He made sure, using his hands, to scrape the bucket clean. He used his tongue where his tongue would reach, not wanting the witch to say he'd left some.

"Well done, man," Rat said.

"Thanks," Brian said, feeling like he was going to burst.

He continued to burp and began passing the most horrendous, nauseating gas he'd ever smelled. Usually, he didn't mind the odor of his own farts, but his latest was cringe worthy. Even Rat backed away, coughing.

Sometime later, Henrietta paid him a visit.

"So, you did it," she said, her expression unreadable, if not with a hint of annoyance.

"We had a deal," Brian said. "I finish and you let me go."

"There was no deal, only what I said. We never agreed on anything."

"Okay," Brian said, holding back his anger, trying to remain calm. "Are you going to let me go?"

"Of course," Henrietta said, a smile that bunched up her cheeks forming across her face. "With the snap of my fingers, you'll be back in your apartment, but first, let me tell you a little something."

CHAPTER 12

BRIAN AWOKE ON his own bed. The change in comfortableness was the first thing he noticed. Next was the odor—cleanliness. It was overwhelming, like waking up on a crisp autumn morning in the Adirondack Mountains.

He sat up and felt his face. Smooth skin, the beard gone. The bed was like a cloud, soft and inviting. Something he never thought he'd experience again.

He took a deep breath and blinked hard as he looked around his room. Everything seemed real, but was it just another trick? Making sure to use his nails, he pinched the flesh on his forearm until it bled. He wasn't dreaming. He was back in his place.

Jumping out of bed, he hooted and hollered. He'd beaten that bitch of a witch. Then, his heart sank a bit at realizing he'd been gone three years—the amount of times he'd fallen asleep.

How was his apartment still his? Wouldn't he have been deemed missing? Dead? But his bedroom looked the same. His cell phone was even charging on the nightstand. Snatching it up, he saw the time was 6 a.m. The date was the same as when he'd left his apartment.

Brian took off to the living room. The body was

gone, as he thought it would be, but so was the blood. The area in front of the recliner was clean. Had he dreamed the whole thing? Had he had some kind of psychotic break? The last thing he remembered was the witch telling him she was sending him back, but cursed. The deal was: until he achieved orgasm with another person, he would puke before coming.

He laughed, nervously. There was no way it could all be real, the puke-eating situation. Besides the whole thing being ridiculous, there were no such things as witches, well, magical ones anyway. And certainly no talking animals.

So how do you explain everything? a voice in his head asked. *Where'd all the blood go?*

He must have dreamed that too. Had not taken a woman home last night.

But it seemed like he had, the memory vivid.

There was only one way to determine the truth, as silly as it was. He hurried to his laptop and logged into his favorite porn site—All Things Go!—and began choking his chicken to an anal pounding scene. It took him a few minutes to fully harden—which worried him a bit—but with his mind all over the place it had taken him time to focus.

As his excitement level increased, the woman on the screen screaming in feigned delight, he heard his stomach gurgle. He kept going, jerking his schlong ferociously and was about to come when a throat-burning throw up burp landed at the back of his throat. He tasted his stomach's vileness. No, not his stomach's vileness, but the witches'. Their vomit was still inside him.

Before he knew it, he was puking all over his laptop, the electronic device caked in slop.

CHAPTER 13

BRIAN STOOD IN the shower, his tears mixing with the water. After ruining his laptop, he'd gone to his desktop computer, chalking up his puking to his mind screwing with him. But after vomiting again shortly before he was about to shoot his load into an aloe-laced tissue, he realized his time in the witch's basement had happened. He may have gotten out of there, but he was far from free.

He remained in his apartment for the next few days, drinking and wallowing in his sorrows. He couldn't get over how he'd never fuck again. Hell, even jerk off. Then one day, after watching CNN's Money Talk, he realized he needed to get off his ass and show that witch he could beat her again. *I mean, look what I did already—eating all that puke. If I did that, I can do anything.*

***

The next night, Brian went out to one of his favorite nightclubs and easily picked up a young woman. She was hot, with a killer body and fake tits—oh, how he loved fake, bouncy tits. He'd hoped to make it home, where he planned on giving it to her good. He wanted her to remember him forever. To long for him when she was married with kids and bored. But as soon as

59

they got in the backseat of the car, she went down on him.

Besides a few times when she used her teeth a little too hard, the blowjob was going well, Brian enjoying himself, until his stomach gurgled and he let forth a stream of nasty-smelling vomit. The woman screamed bloody murder, her curly dark hair weighed down with green muck. When her scream died, she looked at him with fury in her eyes, reached back and punched him in the nose before grabbing her purse and running down the street. Brian ordered his driver to take him home, where he drank himself to sleep.

Two nights later, he picked himself up and tried again. He went to a different nightclub and hooked up with a hot blonde. They started going at it on the dance floor. She rubbed his crotch and made out with him. Their tongues intertwined like snakes in heat. She slid one of her hands down his pants and grabbed his cock. "I want this inside me," she whispered in his ear. They locked lips, and three strokes later, he vomited. She flew backward, puke spewing out of her mouth and falling from her face and chest.

Embarrassed beyond anything he'd ever known before, Brian wasted no time in running. People quickly moved out of his way, so leaving unimpeded wasn't a problem.

As he was driven home, he knew the last two clubs he'd been to were clubs he could never show his face in again.

The next time he tried to have sex was with a hooker, figuring he could simply stick his dick in her and pump away. Blow his load without any foreplay or excitement. He brought the hooker—no streetwalker but a high-end dick blower—to a mid-level hotel and paid her $1,000.00 up front. He instructed her to get on her knees, he would take her from behind. He'd swallowed a Viagra 30 minutes earlier and was rock-hard. Slipping on the condom, he walked up behind her and slid himself in. When she attempted to moan, he told her he wanted her quiet. Not a peep came from the hooker.

As he pounded away, he thought about bugs—spiders and all their gross parts, hoping not to get excited, but quickly realized he would never come that way—especially not with a condom on and a loose pussy with almost no feel to it. He needed to get in the mood, despite his dick being rock-hard. Maybe have her lay on her back so he could look at her tits. No, he'd stay like he was. Instead, he glanced down and stared at her ass and the sexy fairy tattoo above her butt crack. He grabbed hold of her cheeks and squeezed. He was getting into it, ready to come soon. He could feel it. Maybe he'd beaten—

Without warning, his stomach muscles hitched and a stream of orange-colored vomit came forth. It splashed over her back and onto the bed. The woman sprang forward and spun around so she was on her back. "What the fuck?" she said, a mask of utter disgust on her face.

"I'm so sorry—" he began, when she pushed herself forward and kicked him in the chest. He went crashing backwards into the wall and slid to the floor. The hooker jumped up, puke falling off her in mudslide fashion.

"Disgusting," she said and shivered. She stepped up to him with malice in her eyes and a line for a mouth. "I ought to call this in. Have you banned forever. Maybe have the shit beaten out of you." She kicked him in the nuts.

Brian yelped and cupped his balls. "Please, it was an accident," he said.

"Accident my ass," the hooker said. "You rich sickos think you can get away with whatever you want. Well, you're going to pay this time. Three times my usual rate or I tell management. I have to go home and clean up before my next appointment, asshole." She kicked him again, this time in his shin.

Brian agreed to pay her, and as soon as his balls stopped aching, he went to the ATM down the street—leaving his belongings in the room with the hooker—and gave her four times what she wanted, hoping the extra grand would shut her up. She didn't thank him when she counted it, and as she was walking away, she said, "Fucking Emetophiliac. You people make me sick."

As soon as the hooker was gone, Brian got to his feet. His dick was still hard and he pulled the condom off and flung it into the garbage. He sat on the bed and cried, not caring about the puke. If he couldn't come again, life wasn't worth living. It was sad, but part of being a rich and powerful bachelor was the ability to fuck. What would be the point of attracting so many women if he could only be their friend? The world was filled with beautiful women he still hadn't screwed. So many that would be denied his pleasure-giving abilities. It wasn't right. He was a swordless warrior, a conqueror without an army. A has been. A sad sack.

He lay back on the bed, feeling his cold puke mush around him. Then, closing his eyes, he fell asleep.

He awoke an hour later, showered and went home. He couldn't stop seeing the hooker in his mind—a low-life, bottom feeding whore—and how she had treated him. Him!—a successful, wealthy, and incredibly good-looking man. She looked down upon him as if he were nothing but a bug to be squashed, or a homeless beggar to be pissed on. What had she called him? An emetophiliac?

Annoyed she knew a word he did not, he went to his computer and looked up the definition. Emetophelia—a person who was turned on by vomit or the act of vomiting or being vomited on. Holy shit!

He'd heard of watersports and scat play, and knew people did vomit or were vomited on during sex acts, but he didn't know there was a name for such an individual. When he thought about it, he figured why not. There were names and labels for everything. There were all sorts of freaks in the world, and if people enjoyed fucking farm animals, then why wouldn't there be people who enjoyed puking and fucking. Then it hit him like a slap across his face—a way to beat the curse.

He began searching the internet for fetish sites, specifically ones involving puking. Within minutes, he found a number of them. The videos turned his stomach. Pop up windows appeared at the bottom of his screen, people looking to hook up. He began clicking them, most opening new windows that led to other sites. Finally, one led to a message board, and among other messages, there was a section for people looking to hook up with other emetophiliacs. He left a message and his email.

Thirty minutes later, he received an email from PukeLord 666 and nearly lost his lunch when he saw her picture. She had neon green hair, a bone through her nose, and a whitehead-fresh, acne covered forehead. If that wasn't bad enough, the pictures of her vomiting and covered in puke were nauseating. There were even some where she and a few others were smearing what had to be fecal matter all over themselves.

The next email he received was from an anorexic-looking woman who was missing her front teeth. Her eye sockets showed as if the skin were a thin membrane and every one of her ribs were clearly defined against the saggy flesh of her chest. He thought if she puked one more time, she would simply cave in on herself.

He went through a number of emails before he came to one that surprised him. It was from Different 725. She was cute, had an innocent girl next door look. Blonde hair cut with bangs and blue eyes went nicely with her thin but attractive lips. She was almost ordinary, but Brian saw a hint of naughty behind her eyes. A good girl on the outside, bad girl on the inside.

He couldn't believe he'd found her—the perfect puke girl. It was too good to be true. The picture had to be a fake, taken twenty years ago. Some kind of misrepresentation. She was looking for someone to hook up with, for a casual night of vomit-only sex. No scat play or golden showers.

With a pair of sweaty palms, his pulse racing with anticipation, he typed a reply and wrote that he was looking for exactly the same thing. Thirty minutes later, she replied, telling him that she thought he was really hot and looked forward to getting together. They set a time to meet along with a location—the Grand Pavilion Hotel on the East Side of Manhattan.

CHAPTER 14

BRIAN WAITED IN the hotel's lobby, as the pair had agreed. Earlier that morning, the woman sent him an email with the food she wanted to eat. He'd already taken care of that and the booking of the room.

He'd never been as nervous as he currently was—and it pissed him off.

Keeping an eye on the entrance, he saw the woman enter shortly after he had. She looked exactly like her online photo. Wholesome. She was wearing a simple white polka dot red dress that ended just below her knees. From what he could tell, she had little to no makeup on, appearing natural. In a word, she looked pretty.

"Hello," she said, coming up to him and giving a small wave.

Brian stood fast, only realizing it after the fact. He didn't want to appear nervous, like a newbie. "Hi," he said.

"I'm impressed," she said, "you look like your pic."

He smiled. "I was thinking the same thing. What a pleasure."

"Hate it when you meet someone and they look nothing like their pic. Lie from the beginning and I walk."

"Agreed," Brian said, not sure what else to say. He casually rubbed his sweaty hands on his pants.

"What I really mean is you're handsome," she said.

Brian felt a little of his normal swagger come back. "Thank you, and may I say I'm quite happy with what I see."

The woman grinned, her teeth perfectly aligned.

"Shall we?" Brian asked. She nodded and the two headed to the room.

They rode the elevator to the 30th floor. The penthouse Brian reserved was exquisite. It had a Jacuzzi, living room, kitchen, balcony, and bedroom. He knew they wouldn't be enjoying the amenities, at least he wouldn't. Once he shot his load, he was out of there.

The food arrived right after they settled in.

"Looks delicious," the woman said.

"Yes, it does." He wasn't hungry and didn't need to eat in order to puke, but he would eat so he fit in. He excused himself and went to the bathroom where he swallowed a dick-hardening pill. Once the vomiting started, there was no way he would be able to stay hard on his own.

When he returned to the dining area, they ate sesame chicken and broccoli, pea soup and drank glasses of milk. He was amazed at how much she consumed.

"So what should I call you?" he asked, not knowing if real names were shared.

"Naughty Girl," she said right before shoveling food into her mouth. While chewing, she asked, "And you?"

Shit, he had no idea. A normal name would sound lame. "Big. Call me Big."

She giggled. "I hope you live up to it."

"I think you'll be pleased."

"Oh, my God," she said. "All this food, gorging myself, and your name . . . I'm fucking horny as hell." She pushed herself back from the table and stood. "A full tummy always makes me so wet."

Brian swallowed, feeling a small lump in his throat. The woman was scaring him. The change she'd gone through was like something supernatural, from wholesome-next-door-neighbor to wild vixen.

Naughty Girl strode over to him, a sesame seed stuck at the corner of her mouth. She reached down and grabbed his crotch. "Ooh, you weren't kidding, Mr. Big. And it feels like he's ready to be let out."

Brian slid his chair back and stood. His stomach felt as if it had dropped into his groin. His nerves were getting the best of him. But he ignored them. With the Viagra working, he'd be fine.

Naughty Girl led him to the bedroom. She ripped open his button down shirt. Buttons flew about, bouncing over the bed and floor like pearls from a torn necklace. She leaned in and ran her hot tongue up his chest, along his neck and to his lips. They kissed, hands caressing each other. Tongues exploring. She pulled away, put a finger to his lips, winked, and then kissed her way down to his waist. She unbuckled his belt and slid his pants down along with his boxers, revealing his rock-hardness.

Grabbing a hold of it, she said, "I'm going to enjoy gagging on this," and then steered him to the bed. She took him into her warm, moist mouth—all of him. She worked him slowly, up and down, flicking the tip with her tongue before swallowing his shaft up to his balls. Brian's eyes rolled back in his head and he moaned in ecstasy. She gagged whenever she took him all the way in, but seemed to enjoy it.

Brian forgot all about what he was there to do and enjoyed the euphoric blowjob until one of her gags grew thunderous. The pressure of her tight throat was gone the next moment, cool air wafting over his moist cock. He dared a look down, ready to grab her hair and get more, when her body jerked and her mouth opened. A stream of vomit shot forth and covered his penis, balls, and thighs. If it wasn't for the Viagra, his dick would've shriveled to the size of a pea.

Naughty Girl grabbed the slop-covered cock and went back to blowing him. Brian closed his eyes and tried to block out what he'd just seen. Her mouth was like a vacuum, his cock cleaned off within a few blows. But the stench was awful and he could feel his balls shriveling. He breathed through his nose, and for a moment, feared he would still be able to smell the odor of her vomit, but to his pleasant surprise, it worked.

She took his hand and planted it on her head and indicated for him to help her. He obliged and pulled her to him, sending his cock down her throat. He face-fucked her, the puke all but forgotten now. He was getting into it, ready to come, when his stomach gurgled and he let loose a hurl of vomit. The woman's head was draped in tan muck, the sludge dribbling down her back and shoulders. She stopped blowing him and looked up, smiling and moaning. She rubbed the vomit over her chest and neck, smearing it in like lotion. She trembled in ecstasy and he knew she was having an orgasm.

Brian's skin rippled with goosebumps as he fought the urge to vomit again, the sight before him so disgusting he feared he'd have nightmares for the rest of his life. He couldn't comprehend how such an innocent-looking, pretty young woman could be into such a nasty fetish. The "don't judge a book by its cover" never fit so perfectly. People were truly fucked up. This one needed some serious therapy. He was only participating out of a need, had little choice in the matter. And she was passionate about it, loving the puke so much she came.

Naughty Girl stood, more puke dropping off her in clumps. She licked her lips, cleaning off some upchuck. "Yummy," she said, then stripped off her clothes, flinging them to the floor and sending bits of puke onto the walls and television.

Brian was grateful most of the vomit was gone from her person, but her caked hair was still as nasty as before. He thought about telling her to shower off, but knew if he did, he might reveal his true self. He needed to see this through.

Next, she pulled off his upchuck-covered shoes and socks, then his shirt. She shoved him onto the bed, climbed on top of him and lowered herself onto his thickly veined cock. He filled her completely and she moaned with pleasure. As she rode him, he got into it, breathing through his nose and ignoring the horrendous smell, when he realized he wasn't wearing a condom. He opened his mouth to say something—not wanting to get her pregnant or catch some disease—when she stuck her fingers down her throat and vomited on his face. He quickly cleared away as much of the retch as he could, spitting away the stuff that found its way into his mouth. She was riding him hard, coming again. When it was obvious she was done, she kept on, wanting more. She bucked like a wild horse, her perky tits bouncing up and down, nipples stiff. Her vomit strewn hair whipped about, sending vomit everywhere. She took his hands and placed them on her breasts. "Squeeze my nipples, hard." Brian put each one between a forefinger and thumb and squeezed. She bucked harder, ground his cock and yelled, "Fuck me, pig! Fuck me hard. Squeeze my nipples, make them bleed."

At this rate, he was never going to come. He needed not only to take charge, but change the view.

In one practiced move, he grabbed her by her hips and reversed position with her. Now on top, he pumped away, throwing her legs into the air. He held them there, ass up, and filled her with his girth. Her head whipped back and forth as she cried out. "Give it to me. All of it. Fuck me hard. Puke on me. Do it now. I want your hot puke on my tits."

He was feeling it now, staring at her tits and blocking out her puke-covered head. As impossible as it seemed, he was enjoying himself. It felt good knowing that he didn't have to worry about puking. It was expected. She wanted puke, she was going to get it.

He was almost there, ready to blow his load. His stomach gurgled. The next moment, as he slid himself all the way inside her, he vomited all over her chest, splashing her neck and arms and the bed around her. She immediately screamed in pleasure and convulsed with orgasms.

The pleasant view he'd had of her tits was gone, replaced with spilled oatmeal containing peas, carrots, and other things. She was smearing it over herself now, putting her fingers into her mouth. He continued to fuck her, needing to come and figured screwing a rotting corpse might be more pleasant.

Closing his eyes, he imagined Wendy Whoppers, one of his favorite boyhood porn stars. He was fucking her, not Naughty Girl. Naughty Girl's cries of pleasure were Wendy Whoppers'.

His stomach hitched again as he neared orgasm and a long stream of steaming puke spewed forth, splashing Naughty Girl from torso to face. He continued to pump. He puked again. Pumped more. Puked more. Naughty Girl was writhing in pure pleasure, her cries claiming this was the best puke-fuck of her life. Her orgasms matched his puking. The amount of gore covering her was incredible, way more than humanly possible. She didn't seem to care, only basked in its glory. Each vomiting episode let forth a different colored puke and odor. A fog had formed around them, the steaming vomit too much for the air conditioning to clear. The air was thick and he could taste it. He scraped his tongue with his teeth and spit, but it did little to help.

Sweat poured off him as he continued to fuck Naughty Girl. His heart pounded. Determination filled his being. He was a runner nearing the finish line, could feel the ribbon snapping across his chest.

And then, it happened . . .

His balls emptied and he exploded into Naughty Girl, filling her. His own seed covered his cock and poured out of her. Finished, he looked down at her. She was a mummy of puke. He couldn't believe he had been able to come. It proved how truly great he was. He could do anything.

He felt, in a word, better. Like his old self. Something had happened upon ejaculation. Something had come out of him and he knew it was the curse. He felt as if a dark, ominous cloak had been lifted off him.

Realizing he was still inside the woman, he withdrew himself and sat upright.

"Oh, my God," Naughty Girl said. "That was the best puke-fucking I've ever had. Not that I've had a lot with other people, but still . . ."

A chill shot down Brian's spine to his groin. He was beyond disgusted, but at the same time he was proud. He'd really done the impossible, for surely the witch had expected him to fail. To be humiliated for the rest of his life.

Climbing off the bed, he watched the woman sit up. Layers of oatmeal-like mud slathered down her front. Not wanting to look at what he'd fucked, he turned and headed to the bathroom where he took a scalding shower, praying the vomit-loving psycho wouldn't join him.

She didn't.

Back in the room, he dressed in a clean pair of clothes, placing his soiled ones in a plastic bag. Naughty Girl was still on the bed. She was lying in the mess, having smeared it over her body. A solid-looking clump rested on her vagina.

Not wanting to be a complete asshole, he said, "Well, that was fun."

"Yes, it was," she said, moving her arms around in the puke. "I like to lie alone afterward and bask. Feel free to leave."

His type of woman, he thought, then said, "See you," opened the door and left, knowing he would never, ever contact her again. The email he used, everything, would be deleted.

CHAPTER 15

FOR THE MOST PART, Brian's life returned to normal. He had nightmares about his time in the witch's basement. Whenever he had sex, he expected to vomit before he came. Sometimes, he'd get flashbacks of Naughty Girl and her puke-covered body when he was having sex, or he'd think his partner was about to vomit when she was really opening her mouth to scream or moan in pleasure. It was like he was suffering from a form of PTSD.

With therapy, medication, and time, he improved and no longer suffered nightmares involving the witch's basement, or horrifying visions during sex. Fully overcoming his past had only strengthened his resolve at how incredible he was, that he could accomplish and get through anything. Eventually, he was able to put his past behind him.

Then one day, twenty-two years later, Serge the doorman called up to his apartment and informed him that a woman was there to see him. Her name was Jinnie. Brian knew no Jinnie, at least that he could remember, and told Serge so.

"I'm sorry, sir," Serge said, "but she's insistent you see her. Said you'd want to see her. She's the woman you spent time with at the Grand Pavilion some twenty-two years ago."

Panic struck him like an eighteen-wheeler. He froze with the phone to his ear, unable to speak. How the hell had she found him? What the hell could she possibly want?

"Sir?" Serge asked. "Should I send her away?"

"No," Brian blurted. "Send her up." He hung up the receiver and waited by the door.

An unwanted blast from the past.

A minute later, his doorbell rang. Without looking through the peephole, he opened the door. He'd composed himself; had shaken off the nerves by the time she arrived. It was simple. She wanted money. Had discovered he was wealthy and was going to blackmail him. How, he didn't know. Maybe she'd recorded their puke-fucking session. But if she had, then why wait so long to use it?

Looking a bit older, but still pretty, was Naughty Girl. Next to her was a strikingly good-looking young man. It didn't take Brian long to figure out what was going on; the young man looked just like him. A spitting image, in fact.

His mind went back to the night he'd spent at the Grand Pavilion Hotel, a night he thought he'd buried and would never have to rehash again. Part of that memory was that he hadn't worn a condom. He'd exploded inside of her.

Regardless of what he already knew, he'd insist on a DNA test. It was better to be thorough, even though he saw that the young man standing before him was his.

"Hello, Brian," Naughty Girl said.

"Hello, Naught—" He stopped himself,

remembering who Serge had said was there to see him. "Jinnie. It's been a long time."

"Yes," she said, her smile looking forced. "I hadn't planned for this ever to happen, but shit happens. I'm here to tell you that you're a father." She motioned to the young man.

"Hi, Dad," the young man said, his tone sarcastic.

Hearing the word "dad" caused Brian's balls to shrivel to the size of raisins.

"May we come in?" Jinnie asked.

"Um, sure," Brian said, and moved aside.

Finding out he had a child was surreal. Numbing. He would need time, a week maybe, to decide what he was going to do. See if he truly wanted to be a part of the kid's life—a dad—or pay the kid and Jinnie off so he'd never have to see either one of them again.

They sat in the living room. Brian played the role of a good host and got his guests some sodas. He made himself a gin and tonic, heavy on the gin. The young man's name was Kyle. He liked it. It was simple, direct, yet somehow strong and powerful-sounding.

"My mom was on the pill when you guys had your romp, but forgot to take it that night. What were the chances, huh?"

Brian nearly choked on his drink.

"He knows everything," Jinnie said.

"I guess he does," Brian said.

"I need to use the bathroom," Kyle said. "It'll give the adults time to chat freely."

"It's down the hall on the right," Brian said, and waited until he heard the bathroom door close before speaking. "Why did you wait so long to contact me?"

"You were a hook-up," Jinnie said. "Not serious

marrying material. As soon as I found out I was pregnant, I stopped with the whole puke-fucking thing too. Stopped one-night stands in general. I needed to be a responsible mom. I had a great paying job. Still do."

"So, what, Kyle asked who his father is?"

"No. I told him how he was conceived and he was okay with it. A happy boy, until . . ." She sighed.

"Until what?"

"Until his first sexual encounter. He was dating this girl and she decided to blow him one night. He wound up puking on her. Luckily for Kyle, the girl was too embarrassed to tell anyone or his life at school would've been ruined."

Brian didn't know what to say and didn't want to think about it, so he said, "The kid was probably just nervous or had drank too much alcohol."

"That's what I thought, but no. The next girl was a prostitute for his twentieth birthday, his frat brothers getting her for him. He wound up puking on her too."

No, Brian thought. *It can't be.*

"In fact, every person, male or female, cuz he likes them both, that Kyle has tried having sex with he's puked on. I took him to doctors, neuro-specialists, and had him put on medication. Nothing worked. He was distraught, afraid he'd never be able to have sex. Even jerking off to porn proved no good—he puked those times too. He visited alternative methods, saw herbalists and witch doctors and spiritualists. Nothing worked until he found the coven of witches."

Brian was finding it hard to breathe. His past—all of it—had come roaring back. It was then, he knew, that he'd passed his curse on to his son. Shit. If he'd worn a condom, his son wouldn't have been born and the curse not transferred. He could've thrown it away with the condom and his seed.

"It's okay," Brian said. "I know how to get rid of it."

"I know too," Jinnie said, "thanks to my son contacting the witches. It also explains the reason you were with me that night. It explains a lot. Why you weren't as into the puking like others. Why you were acting so weird, like a first-timer. And why you never appeared on the message boards again."

"Kyle just has to blow his load and the curse will leave him. If he does it into a condom, he won't pass it on. I know it'll be difficult, but he can do it. He's my boy, my family's genes are strong."

"You don't think he tried that?" Jinnie asked. "It turns out that since he was born with it there is only one way to get rid of it."

Brian sat forward, eager to hear. "What does he have to do?"

"Kill his maker," Jinnie said.

A hot, stinging pain spread across Brian's throat. Confused, he reached up and felt the area. Warm liquid was splashing over his hands and shirt. Glancing down, he saw the blood decorating him and his floor, gushing like a burst pipe. Trying to draw a breath, he choked and coughed out a mist of crimson that dotted the coffee table. He didn't understand what had happened until he saw Kyle come from around the back of the couch, a bloody knife in his hand.

At that moment, everything clicked for Brian.

Being Kyle's maker, he had to die. And there was nothing he could do now. The wound was mortal.

Paramedics wouldn't be able to save him even if they burst though the door that very moment.

Brian's son and Naughty Girl stood together, her arm snaked around Kyle's waist. They looked happy with one another, like any mother and son should.

With nothing left to do but die, Brian took his last wheeze-filled breath and slumped to the floor dead.

THE END

ABOUT THE AUTHOR

David is originally from a small town in upstate New York called Salisbury Mills. He now resides in NYC and misses being surrounded by chainsaw-wielding maniacs and wild backwoods people who like to eat human flesh. He's grown used to the city, though hiding bodies is much harder there. He is the author of *A Mixed Bag of Blood, Goblins, Skinner, The Unhinged, Witch Island, Fecal Terror, Relic of Death* and others. He is also one of the co-authors of *Jackpot*.

All Art is Junk by R. A. Harris

Lana Rivers, a girl with paintbrush hair, is missing and it's up to Lancelot, her cyborg knight, and his bionic conjoined twin, Cilia, to find her before her evil father, a disrespected artist turned mad-scientist, performs a terrible experiment on her.

Cherub by David C. Hayes

Cherub wasn't like the other boys—too slow, too rough—but he didn't deserve what that hospital did to him, and now he will make them pay.

Skinners by Adam Millard

Los Angeles, the City of Angels. At least, that's what the brochure says. What it fails to mention is the earthquakes. Oh, and the flesh-eating creatures lying dormant beneath the concrete, waiting for the chance to surface once again. Their wait is over . . .

The After-Life Story of Pork Knuckles Malone
by MP Johnson

What's a farm boy to do when his pet pig becomes an evil, decaying hunk of ham with slime-spewing psychic powers?

A Lightbulb's Lament by Grant Wamack

A gentleman with a lightbulb for head wakes up in a world full of darkness, hooks up with a beautiful ex-prostitute, and an old man who can heal people; he travels down south to find the mysterious Creator.

PseudoPsalms by Peter Adam Saloman

Bram Stoker nominated author Peter Adam Salomon has laid bare the intricate horrors of the human condition in this poetic compilation; PseudoPsalms: Saints v. Sinners.

Gravity Comics Massacre
by Vincenzo Bilof

An absolutely shitty novella involving comic books, aliens, a serial killer, teenagers in an abandoned town, horror-trope dream sequences, and an ending you're going to hate.

Glue by Scott Lange

Sticky bowels and sticky situations.

Ascent by Matthew Bialer

Is the 8 foot tall creature haunting a small town in Iowa in the fall of the year 1903 the product of a hoax and collective imagination or was it one of the first documented paranormal event in America? This epic poem grapples with these questions.

Fecal Terror by David Bernstein

A killer turd is on the loose!

The Fairy Princess of Trains
by Christopher Boyle

Danny's mediocre life turns upside-down when his couch starts whispering to him. Then he's charged with a supernatural mission: Rescue the Fairy Princess of Trains.

Terence, Mephisto & Viscera Eyes
by Chris Kelso

9 new science fiction stories from Chris Kelso

Bizarro Bizarro: An Anthology

The finest bizarro short stories from 2013.

Notes from the Guts of a Hippo
by Grant Wamack

A rugged journalist travels to Brazil in search of a missing hippo researcher and the notes left behind lead to something earth shatteringly revelatory.

Day of the Milkman by S. T. Cartledge

In a world dominated by the milk industry, only one milkman survives after a terrible storm sinks all the ships and throws the Great White Sea out of balance.

Moosejaw Frontier by Chris Kelso

An unapologetic disaster of metafiction

Notes from the Guts of a Hippo
by Grant Wamack

A rugged journalist travels to Brazil in search of a missing hippo researcher and the notes left behind lead to something earth shatteringly revelatory.

Industrial Carpet Drag by Bruce Taylor

Chemicals make you do great things!

Necrosaurus Rex by Nicolas Day

Necrosaurus Rex tells the tale of Martin, a simple janitor, who takes an unfortunate trip through time, becomes a violent mutant, and the father of us all. There's 14 billion years crushed inside these pages, and most of them are pretty nasty.

The Boy Who Loved Death by Hal Duncan

From blackest humour to bleakest horror, with twisted relish, Hal Duncan's eighteen tales dig into death—and the life that goes with it.

X's for Eyes by Laird Barron

Between the machinations of the disciples of black gods and good old corporate skullduggery, it's winding up to be of a hell of a summer vacation for the Tooms Brothers.

Omega Grey by Seb Doubinsky

When professor Todd Bailer embarked on a psychedelics quest to discover if the land of the Dead really existed, he had no idea he would threaten the cosmic balance of the universe by triggering a real-estate conquest of the new Frontier.

Berzerkoids by MP Johnson

The first short story collection from Wonderland Book Award-winning author MP Johnson

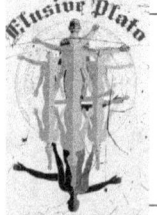

Elusive Plato by Rhys Hughes

The last in a long decadent line of piratical Spanish eccentrics, Bartleby Cadiz grows up in isolation to be as mad, bad and metaphysical as his ancestors. But he feels there is something different about him. What can it be?

Boiled Americans
by Matthew Allen Rose

Boiled Americans is a puzzle box in book form, inspired by the violence of living in urban America and exploding the tendency to forget or ignore.

Great American Slasher
by David C. Hayes

Baseball, apple pie . . . and murder.

The Bohemian Guide to Monogamy
by Andrew Armacost

Here, a strange labyrinth of interlinked short fiction assembles itself into a darkly moving novella that deftly explores the bottomless pain and pleasure of love and commitment.

Surreal Worlds edited by Sean Leonard

An anthology of surrealistic compositions created by some of the finest names in genre fiction. A showcase of international talent undaunted by the conventions of language and common narrative structures. Here is timelessness. Here is Surreal Worlds

How to Succesfully Kidnap Strangers
by Max Booth III

Do not respond to bad reviews. If you must respond to bad reviews, please do not kidnap the reviewer.

ADHD Vampire by Matthew Vaughn

He came, he conquered, he was distracted a lot